THIS BOOK BELONGS TO

........................................................

# PUSS IN BOOTS

Written by Helen Anderton

Illustrated by Stuart Lynch

make
believe
ideas

# Reading together

This book is designed to be fun for children who are gaining confidence in their reading. They will enjoy and benefit from some time discussing the story with an adult. Here are some ways you can help your child take those first steps in reading:

* Encourage your child to look at the pictures and talk about what is happening in the story.

* Help your child to find familiar words and sound out the letters in harder words.

* Ask your child to read and repeat each short sentence.

## Look at rhymes

Many of the sentences in this book are simple rhymes. Encourage your child to recognize rhyming words. Try asking the following questions:

* What does this word say?

* Can you find a word that rhymes with it?

* Look at the ending of two words that rhyme. Are they spelled the same? For example, "plan" and "man," and "too" and "true."

# Reading activities

The **What happens next?** activity encourages your child to retell the story and point to the mixed-up pictures in the right order.

The **Rhyming words** activity takes six words from the story and asks your child to read and find other words that rhyme with them.

The **Key words** pages provide practice with common words used in the context of the book. Read the sentences with your child and encourage him or her to make up more sentences using the key words listed around the border.

A **Picture dictionary** page asks children to focus closely on nine words from the story. Encourage your child to look carefully at each word, cover it with his or her hand, write it on a separate piece of paper, and finally, check it!

Do not complete all the activities at once – doing one each time you read will ensure that your child continues to enjoy the story and the time you are spending together. Have fun!

A mean old miller died one day,
and written in his will,
he gave two sons the house and horse,
while the cat was left to Bill.

Bill asked his brothers, "Can't you help?"
    (He was in a tricky spot.)
But they said, "Go! And take that cat,"
    leaving Bill with not a lot.

7

Bill said, "Oh, what can I do?
Perhaps I'll eat my cat!"
But the crafty cat, on hearing this,
said, "Hey! Please don't do that!"

Said Puss, "Buy me a bag and boots –
I'll make your dreams come true.
Trust me, and I will bring you gold,
and a wife and a palace, too."

Thrilled, Bill found a bag and boots.
Then Puss said, "Here's the plan:
We'll take some gifts to please the king –
and make you a wealthy man."

Puss caught a rabbit in the bag,
and then he made a stew.
"I'll take this to the king," he said,
"and say it comes from you."

Puss gave many gifts this way –
delivering them by hand.
He told the king, "They're from Lord Stone!"
(To make young Bill sound grand.)

"Now," Puss said, "trust me once more.
Go take a morning swim."
And while Bill swam, Puss stole his clothes —
which put Bill in a spin!

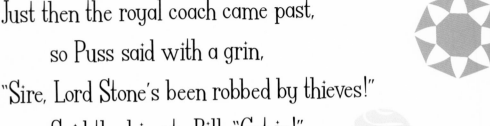

Just then the royal coach came past,
    so Puss said with a grin,
"Sire, Lord Stone's been robbed by thieves!"
    Said the king to Bill, "Get in!"

The princess gave Bill smart new clothes,
    and to thank her for this kindness,
Puss said, "Sire, at Lord Stone's home
    we have a feast for you and Her Highness!"

Puss had one thing left to do.
He ran ahead to find
a palace lived in by a troll –
the mean and nasty kind.

ROAR!

This troll could change into a bee,
a lion, or a seal.
Puss thought, "If I can trick the troll,
his palace is mine to steal."

Said Puss, "Now, Troll, I hear it's true
you can be a lion or bee.
I picture you as a fierce beast,
but it's a MOUSE I'd like to see."

With that, the troll became a mouse –
right there on the floor!
In a flash, Puss ate him up
and wrote "Lord Stone" on the door.

Lord Stone

Puss stood proudly at the door
as the royal coach arrived.
The king was amazed and said to Bill:
"Take my daughter as your bride!"

Bill had all that he could want
with a palace and his wife.
And Puss in Boots was free to live
a long and happy life!

# What happens next?

Some of the pictures from the story have been mixed up! Can you retell the story and point to each picture in the correct order?

Lord
Stone

# Rhyming words

Read the words in the middle of each group and point to the other words that rhyme with them.

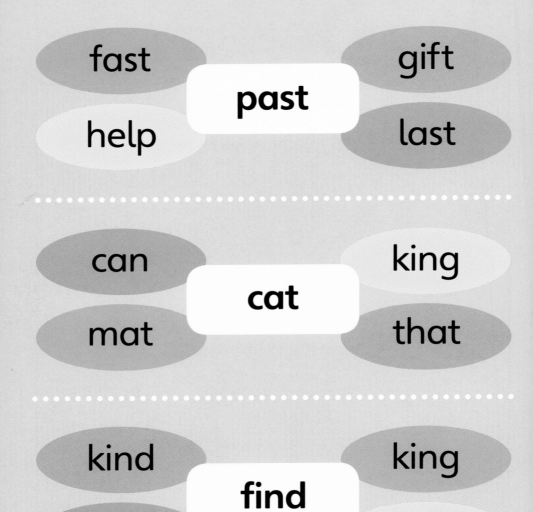

fast

gift

**past**

help

last

can

king

**cat**

mat

that

kind

king

**find**

mind

troll

puss

rabbit

**seal**

real

steal

door

see

**bee**

stew

tea

knife

life

**wife**

lion

boots

Now choose a word and make up a rhyming chant!

I **see** a **bee** drinking **tea!**

# Key words

These sentences use common words to describe the story. Read the sentences and then make up new sentences for the other words in the border.

Bill **is** given a cat.

The cat asks Bill **for** a bag and boots.

Puss in Boots says he will **help** Bill.

Puss gives a rabbit **to** the king.

**Then** he steals Bill's clothes!

like · very

· are · but · saw · with · all · we · help · his · go · not

**The** princess gives Bill new clothes.

Puss finds **a** troll's palace.

**He** tricks the troll.

Puss writes "Lord Stone" **on** the door.

Bill is **very** happy!

the · and · got · to · had · in · he · I · of · it · went · a · they · on · she · is · for · at

could · when · there · put · this · then · so · back ·

# Picture dictionary

Look carefully at the pictures and the words.
Now cover the words, one at a time.
Can you remember how to write them?

bag

boots

coach

gold

palace

rabbit

stew

troll

wife